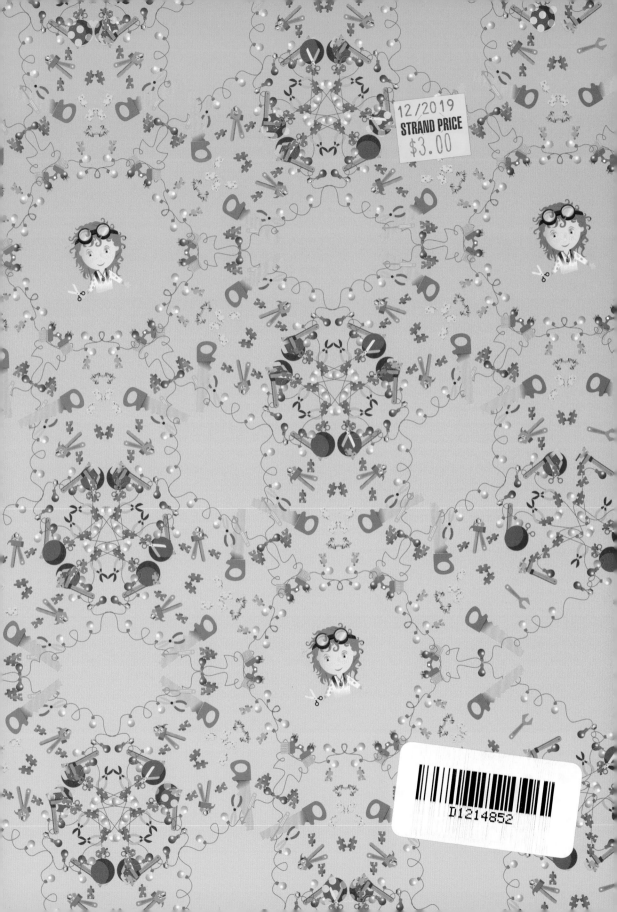

For all children

For all parents...
only if they behaved well.

For Ángel, Eli and Shaya.

Benoliel, Keren
Lupita and her friend Ruby the inventor
by Keren Benoliel;
- 1st ed.
Ciudad Autónoma Buenos Aires : Keren Benoliel, 2018.
44 p. : il. ; 243 x 180 mm. (La petite tortue)

Translated by: Abigail Sofer Levi

ISBN 978-987-42-9663-4

1. Children's literature. I. Turdera, Cristian, ilus. II. Titre. CDD 843.9282
©2018, Keren Benoliel © Original idea and text: Keren Benoliel

Artistic direction & Publisher: Keren Benoliel

Editorial coordinator: Diego Torrendell

Illustrated by: Cristian Turdera

Graphic Designer: ben@bensimon.fr

Edited by: Julie Apfel

www.editionsqueltoupet.com

Printed in Argentina by: TRIÑANES S.A
First edition: December 2018

LUPITA

and her friend Ruby the inventor

RUBY

The inventor

Ingenious, bright and determined.
That's our little Ruby!
Can you guess her favourite hobby?
Making things in her wooden tree house,
a playhouse nestling high up in the
branches.
And that is where she likes to spend her
time, quietly working on her genius
inventions...or almost genius.

"Come on, let's go! Come on, Ruby! Come down! I'll take you to the zoo! They've just welcomed a new resident! A camel with two humps!" shouts Lupita loudly, standing at the foot of the tree to make sure she's heard.

From the back of her tree house comes Ruby's immediate reply as she shouts back:
"Thank you, Lupita! But I'm busy, and the truth is, what do I care if it has two humps or six! Besides, camels have the smelliest breath! They stink!"
"That's true! They certainly don't seem to use toothpaste!" says Lupita laughing. "Well then, let me suggest another idea. Let's go to the cinema! They're showing **Alice in Turtle Wonderland** and my cousin is playing the lead role!"
"I'm very happy for your cousin! But as I just told you, I'm busy" answers Ruby adding, a little rudely perhaps, "and your cousin, she stinks, too - she smells of feet!"

zdoing

zdoing

"You're absolutely right, she does! In Mother Turtle's holey tights' name! Her fat, chubby feet do smell like cheese - like *Camembert* cheese!!" replies Lupita, bursting with laughter.
"Well, well, well, now I understand! *Mademoiselle* Ruby is in the middle of making something in her hideout. Isn't that so?" shouts up Lupita.

Heellooo !!!

... Nothing. There is no reply.

"Heelloooo! Is there anybody up there? Ma-de-moi-sellleee Ru-byyyyyy...!" Lupita yells up once again, trying to convince her friend to come down. "Fine, I'll stop shouting like a crazy turtle! Send me the bucket please - I'm coming up to see you!" says Lupita, now shouting even louder.

Ruby, sitting in her tree house with a small steel screw clamped between her lips, finally gets up and comes to the window. Using the strong rope attached to it, she throws Lupita the big bucket: her famous **ele-bucket-or,** one of her finest creations. Lupita gets in, holds on tight to the rope and closes her eyes to shut out her terrible fear of heights.

Hooo...ist! Hooo...ist!

Carefully and without having to use too much strength, Ruby hauls in the bucket, winching up her friend before hoisting her on to the balcony.

Hooo...ist! Hooo...ist!

"Am I there yet? Can I open my eyes now?" asks Lupita, white as a sheet.

"Yes, don't you worry, my little scaredy-cat. Just hold my hand," Ruby tells her, calming her down.

Hop! Lupita jumps out of the bucket and directly into Ruby's arms, flinging herself around her friend's neck. Ruby in turn scoops Lupita up and carries her into the tree house.

Our little turtle is the only one allowed to visit when Ruby-recycle-everything's creative spirit is in action. What a joy, what a pleasure it is for Lupita to share those special moments up there in the tree!
In the tree house, everything is pleasant: the delicious scent of the cedar that perfumes the air and the drip-drop of the morning dew plinking *staccato* over the wood like a prelude on a harpsichord.

Plic. Ploc. Plic. Ploc.

In one corner of the sturdy wooden tree house sits a big, round armchair - as round as a macaroon. And there are shelves piled high with paraphernalia, groaning under the weight of toolboxes filled to the brim. There is everything you can imagine: screws, screws and more little screws, pliers, wire, pins, scissors, rope, paper, cartons, little old rusty clocks...not forgetting the multi-coloured fairy lights that glow at night and recharge during the day thanks to the sun. Another one of Ruby's great ideas!

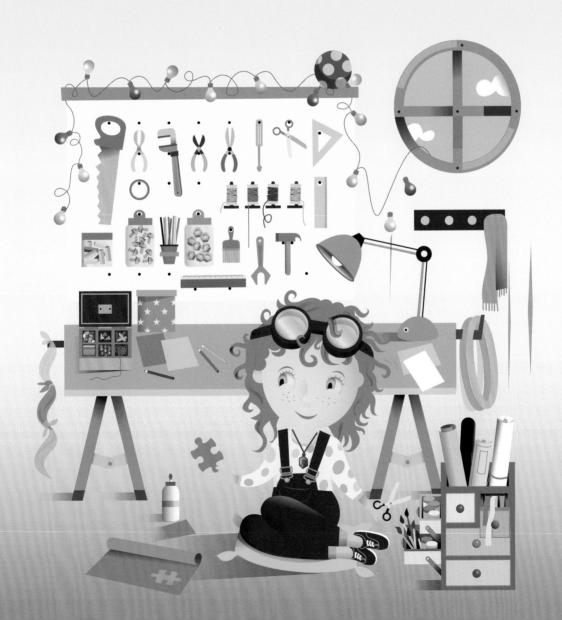

But not all her ideas are that great. Some of them can be surprisingly funny. Like that one time she made helmets out of pasta strainers decorated with multi-coloured butterflies for her friends.

"Don't you remember, Ruby?" asks Lupita.

"Yes, of course!" says Ruby laughing. "And I even remember that I forgot to tell them not to use them in the rain. **And Splash! Splish! Splosh!** Everyone ended up completely soaked from head to toe when it started raining cats and dogs."

"Oh Ruby, my Ruby, you are truly so funny!" Lupita exclaims. "But let's get back to our turtles, as my grandmother would say... Why don't you want to go for a stroll?... Ahhh! But of course, now I understand! IN-CRE-DIB-LE!" she cries, suddenly noticing the unfinished work in the middle of the room.

"You still haven't finished your present for your grandpa's birthday!"

"Yes, that's exactly it, my dear Lupita. The big party is tomorrow and look: what a total mess!" replies Ruby.

For some weeks now, Ruby has been preparing a magnificent gift for her grandfather, who she has always admired.

A great adventurer throughout his life, her grandpa, **Gaspard-Léon de Grossouliers,** travelled across oceans, continents, mountains, jungles and deserts. Not to mention his fantastic voyage through the Mountain of Joy when he brought back not a joy, but a jewel: a ruby in the shape of a smiley face. This very treasure, now hanging from a necklace Ruby never takes off, is where our precious, brilliant friend got her name.

So now you might understand why, for his birthday, Ruby, in turn, wanted to give him an equally unique and precious gift.

Keeping the present top secret, she set out to make what would surely be the greatest masterpiece of her entire childhood. In a labour of overflowing love, Ruby started to create a puzzle in the form of a globe, soon to become a replica of planet Earth.

And yes, **Gaspard-Léon,** once tall, robust and handsome, today because of his age can unfortunately no longer embark on the odysseys he enjoyed in his earlier years.

But thanks to his granddaughter's inspired creation, he will now once again be able to travel the world as many times as his heart desires. All he will have to do is spin her **genius puzzle** round and round on his fingertips and he'll be on his way. Ruby, swept up by her vivid imagination, visualised him doing just that:

"Lupita, do you realise, Grandpa **Gaspard-Léon** is going to be able to take all the trips of his dreams?!" exclaimed Ruby.

"A trip to infinity," sighs Lupita, now excitedly sharing her friend's vision. "Your gift is magical. You're a genius!"

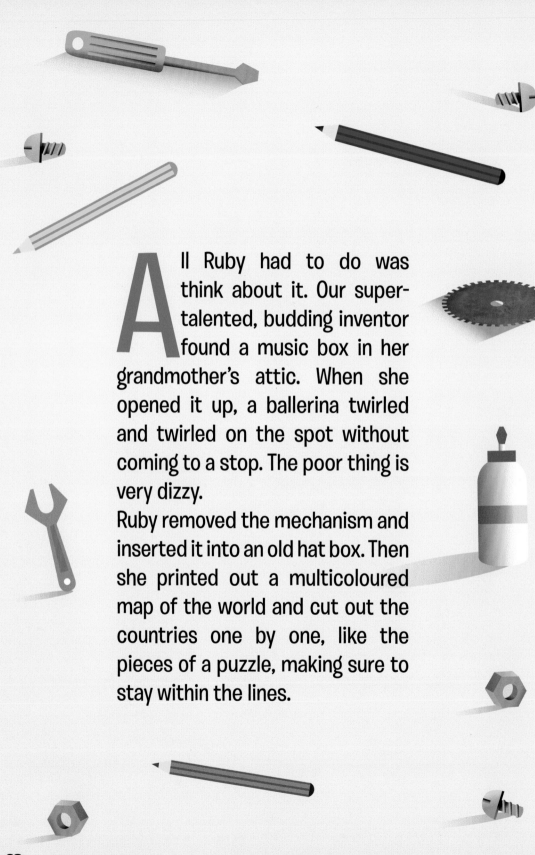

All Ruby had to do was think about it. Our super-talented, budding inventor found a music box in her grandmother's attic. When she opened it up, a ballerina twirled and twirled on the spot without coming to a stop. The poor thing is very dizzy.

Ruby removed the mechanism and inserted it into an old hat box. Then she printed out a multicoloured map of the world and cut out the countries one by one, like the pieces of a puzzle, making sure to stay within the lines.

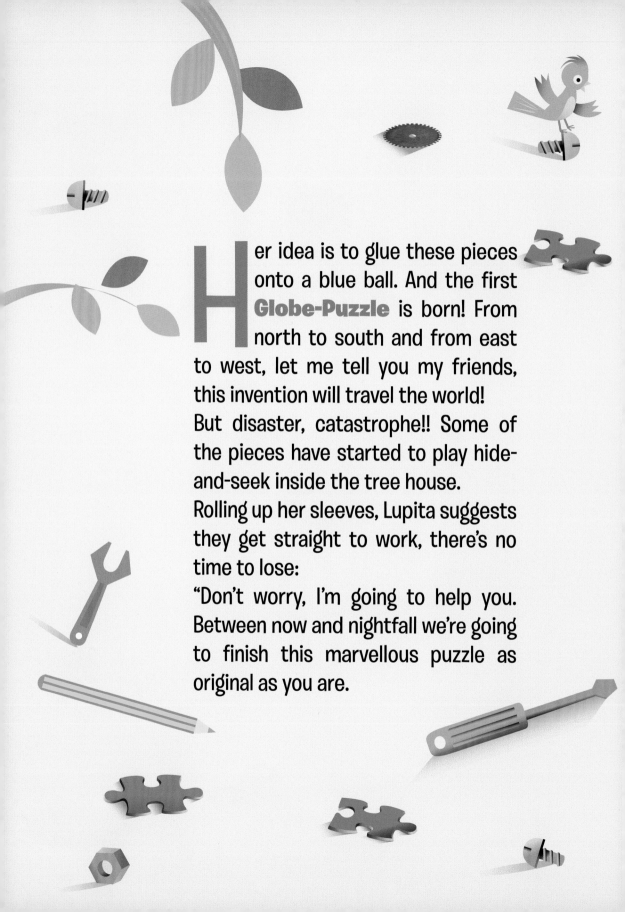

Her idea is to glue these pieces onto a blue ball. And the first **Globe-Puzzle** is born! From north to south and from east to west, let me tell you my friends, this invention will travel the world!

But disaster, catastrophe!! Some of the pieces have started to play hide-and-seek inside the tree house.

Rolling up her sleeves, Lupita suggests they get straight to work, there's no time to lose:

"Don't worry, I'm going to help you. Between now and nightfall we're going to finish this marvellous puzzle as original as you are.

Let's see... hmm... what are we missing?"

Lupita, an expert in geography, first checks which countries are absent from the globe.

"Now, let's go find them," said Lupita. "Ahoy there! Land of the Incas, where are you? Come out of your hiding place! Yoo-hoo! Cu-ckoo! Per-uuu!" called Lupita, checking through the list of missing countries whilst Ruby searched the room.

But the workshop was in such a higgledy-piggledy, mishmash jumble that they couldn't spot the puzzle pieces among the scraps of paper, toy parts, drawings and other small strange, very bizarre objects lying on the floor. Bizarre, did you say bizarre? How bizarre!

Lupita's gaze sweeps the tree house and what does she see? The Land of Llamas hiding in a cosy nest - **a chullo,** Ruby's favourite peruvian hat.

Plop! A little blob of glue and hey presto, it's stuck onto the Globe-Puzzle.

"And **Mongolia?** Can you see it?" asks Lupita.

"Let me think," answers Ruby.

She looks up towards the sky and *voilà!* There it is! **The Land of Blue Sky** is stuck to the ceiling like a butterfly. The puzzle is almost finished. Ruby jumps with joy.

"My, oh my, you jump so high! You'd think we were in The Land of Kangaroos. And look at that, we're still missing Australia," says Lupita knowingly.

A gentle breeze suddenly drifts in through the window, caressing our ingenious little friend's red Land of Fire-y hair. Wow! **Tierra del Fuego** and the Land Down Under are now peeping through.

"I've found them!" exclaims Lupita excitedly.

"What?" asks Ruby.

Lupita deftly removes the two jigsaw pieces from Ruby's tousled hair.

"Ah, the two little players were there all along: Ushuaia and Australia. Bingo! Now we've finally got them!" cries Ruby.

Holding the two pieces in her hands, Ruby heads towards the Globe. Kerplunk! She slips on a pile of pearls and falls, landing straight on her backside. Yikes! But no harm done!

"What pretty pearls!" says Lupita enthusiastically. "Where do they come from?"

"From Madagascar. Grandpa **Gaspard-Léon** brought them back for me on his last trip," explains Ruby.

"Let's see, wait a minute! Madagascar can't be too far from here then. And yes, *voilà,* here it is!" cries Lupita, "the piece is in the middle of Pearl Island!"

What an adventure, my friends.

We're almost there - only one country left to find: **Japan.**

But the time has flown by so fast that it's almost nightfall. In a short while we will hardly be able to see anything. The fairy lights turn on and a soft, warm light envelopes our two friends, both of them now tired out after their thrilling game of hide-and-seek. Lupita and Ruby, yawning like hippopotamuses, fall fast asleep on the floor.

Ssssshhhhh!

At dawn the chatter of parrots wakes our two friends. A ray of sunlight tickles Ruby's eyelids, slowly forcing open her big, mischievous eyes. At **Sunrise** she is astonished to see a small puzzle piece appear. And yes, of course, it couldn't be any other than our dear **Japan.**

Delighted, Lupita wiggles inside her shell. She walks towards Ruby and together they wrap the gigantic gift.
Good to go, Lupita and Ruby walk happily hand in hand to Grandpa Gaspard-Léon the Great's birthday party.

Count to three and blow hard:
1... 2... 3...

The Quel Toupet ! Library

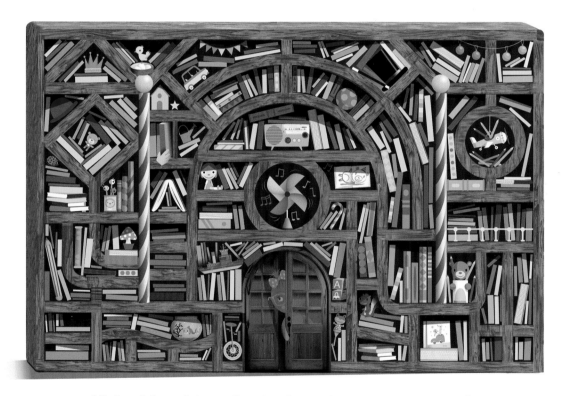

All the titles of the collection *La petite tortue* are available
in 🇫🇷 **French** (original texts) and in 🇪🇸 **Spanish**,
published by *Les Éditions Quel Toupet !*

Collection
La petite tortue

In the same collection

LUPITA and her friend Stan the sweet tooth
LUPITA and her friend Archie the artist
LUPITA and her friend Torvic the athlete
LUPITA and her friend Iris the intellectual
LUPITA and her friend Leonora the romantic

Les éditions
Quel
Toupet !